# Bully for the Beast!

**For a free color catalog describing Gareth Stevens' list of high-quality children's books, call 1-800-341-3569 (USA) or 1-800-461-9120 (Canada).**

**For more stories about the Beast, see**

***The Beast in the Bathtub***
***The Beast and the Babysitter***

**Library of Congress Cataloging-in-Publication Data**

Stevens, Kathleen.
Bully for the beast!

Summary: Lewis's monster friend the Beast helps him enjoy a day at the beach, building a fort in the sand and avoiding the unwelcome attentions of noisy Max.
[1. Beaches—Fiction. 2. Monsters—Fiction] I. Bowler, Ray, ill. II. Title.
PZ7.S84454Bu 1989 [E] 88-33090
ISBN 0-8368-0020-6

First published in 1990 by

**Gareth Stevens Children's Books**
RiverCenter Building, Suite 201
1555 North RiverCenter Drive
Milwaukee, Wisconsin 53212, USA



Art direction: Kate Kriege
Editor: Rhoda Irene Sherwood

Printed in the United States of America

1 2 3 4 5 6 7 8 9 96 95 94 93 92 91 90

# Bully for the Beast!



Story by Kathleen Stevens
Illustrated by Ray Bowler

Gareth Stevens Children's Books
**MILWAUKEE**

Lewis hopped off the edge of the parking lot onto the beach.

"Let's put the blanket over there," said his mother.

As Lewis and his mother spread the blanket, a boy in red bathing trunks ran by, kicking sand in all directions. "Beep-beep!" he shouted. "Make way for Max the Truck."

Lewis's mother brushed sand off his little sister, Meggie. "Someone ought to give Max the Truck a traffic ticket," she said.

"Can I go swimming now?" asked Lewis.

"Stay near the lifeguard," said his mother.

As Lewis waded into the chilly water, the boy in red bathing trunks returned. "Var-o-o-m, var-o-o-m!" he cried. "I'm Max the Truck!" He stomped his feet, splashing everyone he passed.

Lewis shivered and ran into a deep wave. Something scaly brushed his ankle. A bristly green head broke through the surface.

"Hello, Beast!" said Lewis. "How's the water?"

The Beast blew a bubbly grin.

"I don't know whether Beasts are allowed at the beach," Lewis told him. "We'd better hide."

Lewis slid onto the Beast's back, and the Beast paddled behind the rocks.

"I'll bring my bucket and shovel," said Lewis. "We can build a sand fort."

Lewis's mother looked up from her knitting. "Back already from your swim?"

"I'm going to build a fort in the rocks," said Lewis. He rubbed his stomach. "People get hungry building forts, you know."

His mother took out her change purse. "Maybe a Popsicle will help."

"I think it will," said Lewis.

The ice-cream man opened his freezer. "What flavor, sonny?"

Lewis chose orange. Orange was Lewis's favorite flavor. The Beast's too.

Lewis broke the Popsicle down the middle and carried both halves back to the rocks. "Look what I have, Beast," he said.

Lewis licked <u>his</u> Popsicle. The Beast had a better idea. He opened his mouth and slid the Popsicle inside. Slur-r-r-rp. Out came the bare stick. The Beast opened his mouth again.

"Don't eat the stick!" cried Lewis. "We'll use the sticks for flagpoles."

Lewis marked out a space for the fort. The Beast plowed up piles of damp sand, and Lewis shaped the sand into walls and towers. He planted Popsicle-stick flagpoles in the highest towers. It was a splendid fort.

The Beast yawned sleepily.

"You can take a nap while I dig a moat around the fort," said Lewis. "I'll cover you with sand so you don't get sunburned."

Lewis shoveled sand over the Beast's scaly back and bristly head. He left two holes so the Beast could breathe. Then Lewis began to dig the moat.

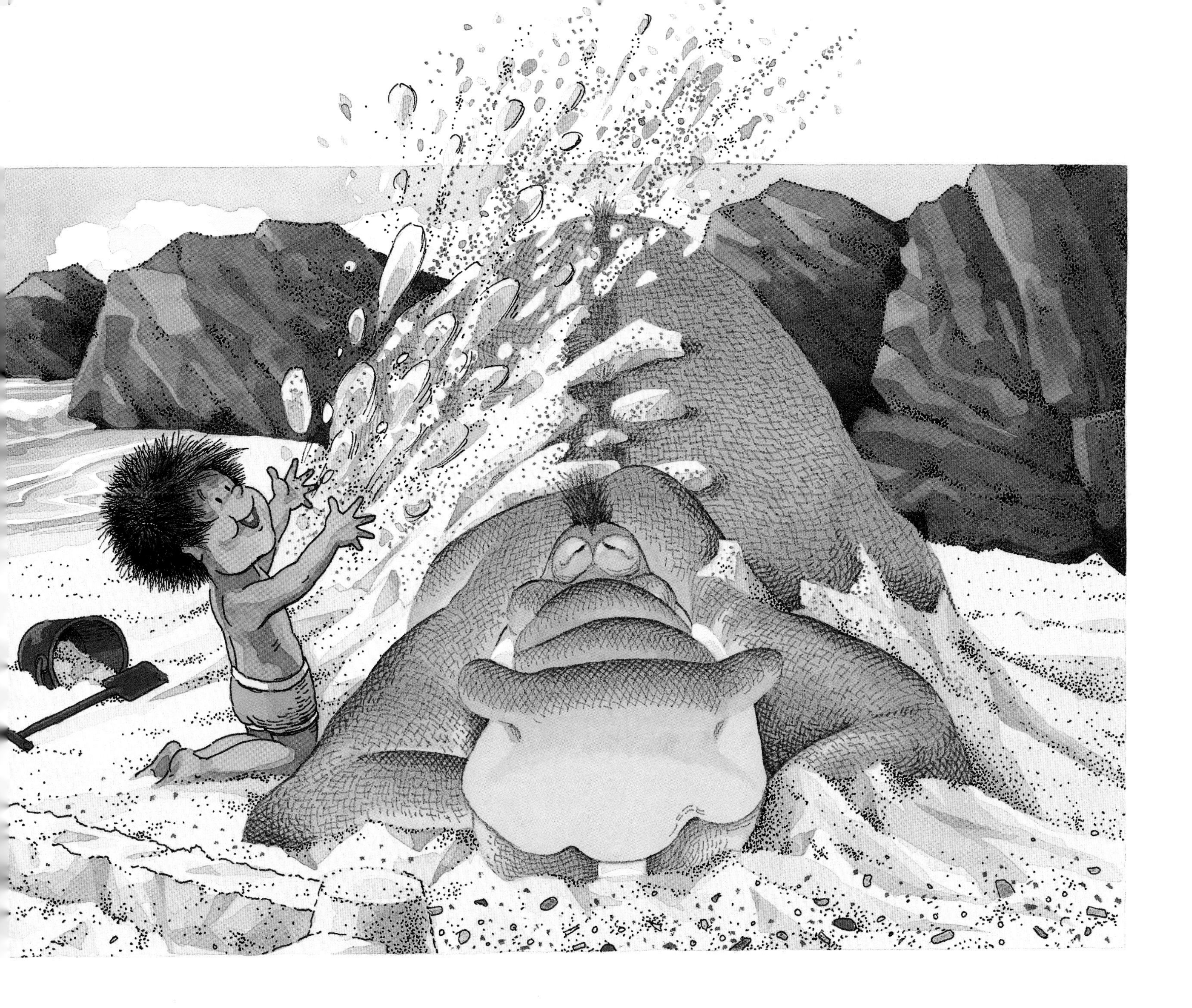

"Here you are!" said Max the Truck. "I've been looking for you. I want your rubber raft."

"I don't have a raft," said Lewis.

"Don't kid me!" growled Max. "I saw you paddling on that big green raft. Give me that raft or else."

"Or else what?" asked Lewis.

"Or else this . . ." Max kicked a hole in the fort.

"Stop!" Lewis protested.

"Make me." Max kicked another hole. "I'm Max the Truck, and I do what I want."

Lewis tried to pull Max away from the fort. Max put his head down and butted Lewis in the stomach. "This is your last chance," he growled. "Give me that raft."

Lewis shook his head.

Max trampled down the whole fort. He even broke the Popsicle sticks. Then he leaped onto the mound of sand and glared at Lewis. "Give me that raft or I'll stomp on you!"

The mound of sand stirred under Max's feet. "Whoa!" cried Max, waving his arms. Thump! Max toppled off and landed in a heap. The mound split apart, and the Beast blinked at Max.

"You want my raft?" said Lewis. "Here it is."

Max stared at the Beast. The Beast stared back, grinning. Max backed away on his hands and knees. The Beast followed, thumping his forked tail.

"He-e-lp!" said Max. He scrambled to his feet and ran off through the rocks.

Lewis rubbed the Beast's scaly head. "I guess Max changed his mind about wanting my raft. But I'll bet he'll be back. You'd better hide."

Max came back, all right — and brought the lifeguard with him.

"That Beast was right here!" shouted Max. "He was huge and scaly and horrible. He tried to eat me!"

The lifeguard scratched his head. "Have you seen a Beast around here?" he asked Lewis.

"A horrible Beast? A Beast that eats kids? No," said Lewis.

Max's face turned red. "That Beast was here! I'm Max the Truck, and I saw him."

"You've been in the sun too long, Max," said the lifeguard. "Your engine's boiling over. Let's go find your mother."

The lifeguard hauled Max away, still sputtering, "I saw that Beast. I did. . . . I did!"

"Lewis," called his mother. "Time to leave."

Lewis followed his mother and Meggie up to the parking lot. He brushed off his sandy feet and climbed into the back seat of the car. His mother started the engine.

And then . . .

. . . they all drove home.